THE SCIENCE AND STORY OF
TITANIC

BY SUSAN HUGHES AND STEVE SANTINI   ILLUSTRATED BY MARGO DAVIES LECLAIR

SOMERVILLE HOUSE, USA

TABLE OF CONTENTS

[Previous page] *White Star Line officer's button*

ICEBERG AHEAD!

By the time they saw it, it was too late. Frederick Fleet and Reginald Lee were lookouts on the gigantic ocean liner RMS *Titanic*. Stationed in the crow's-nest on the ship's foremast, the two men were nearing the end of their watch. Perhaps they rubbed their eyes to relieve the strain of peering out into the blackness of the night. They had no binoculars. These had been left behind in the flurry of excitement as the greatest ship ever to sail the seas began its maiden voyage.

Certainly Fleet and Lee were tired and very cold. The air temperature on this April evening was a freezing 32°F (0°C), only one degree warmer than the deep North Atlantic waters beneath the ship. In half an hour, it would be midnight, and the lookouts' watch would be over. The men could climb down to the deck and head into the warmth of the ship. Until then, Fleet and Lee knew they were to be on the alert for icebergs.

The *Titanic* had received warnings from other ships that icebergs had been seen in the area. However, conditions for spotting icebergs were not ideal. The sky was clear and the stars were out, but there was no wind. The sea was absolutely calm. No waves would kick up a white, warning surf around the base of the icebergs, signaling their location to the lookouts.

It was 11:35 P.M. Suddenly, Fleet's heart began to pound. What was that? What was that shape, that dark shape, appearing out there where only sea should be?

It could be only one thing. Acting quickly and following standard shipboard procedure, Fleet reached for the crow's-nest bell. He rang it hard. Once — then again — then again. Three rings were a warning to the bridge that an object had been sighted dead ahead. Fleet then grabbed the telephone that connected the crow's-nest to the *Titanic*'s bridge, from which the ship was navigated. "Iceberg right ahead!" he said urgently.

Frederick Fleet hung up the phone. His eyes, and Lee's, had not left the ominous shape. It was growing larger and larger. It seemed to the men that the iceberg was coming toward the *Titanic*, but they knew it was the ship that was steaming, at almost full speed, toward the massive

wall of ice directly ahead.
In less than a minute, the
world changed forever —
for Fleet, for Lee, and for the
other 2,226 crew members and
passengers aboard the *Titanic*.

WAVES OF WARNING

Today, radar and sonar systems give officers on the bridge of a ship advance warning of objects both above and below the surface of the water. Radar sends out pulses of high-frequency radio waves above the water. Sonar sends out underwater sound waves. When these waves collide with an object, they bounce back, letting crew members know that there is an obstacle ahead.

Lookout Frederick Fleet climbed the iron ladder inside the Titanic's *foremast. He reached the steel crow's-nest, 95 feet (29 m) above the water, and at 10:00 P.M. on April 14, 1912, his shift began.*

RMS TITANIC

The early 1900s were a time of great scientific invention. One success after another created a mood of optimism. In 1895, Guglielmo Marconi invented radio transmission.

In 1908, Henry Ford began mass-producing cars. One year later, Louis Blériot made the first flight across the English Channel. Bigger, faster, higher — nothing seemed beyond the reach of science.

And then came the *Titanic*. It was the largest ocean liner of its day — 100 feet (30 m) longer and 15,000 tons (13 600 t) heavier than any other ship. The most modern technology was used to build it. The most up-to-date devices were used to meet every safety regulation. No expense was spared.

For three years, from March 1909 to April 1912, an enthralled public in North America and Europe watched as the great ship was built, launched, and made ready for its first voyage. Dazzled by scientific progress, many onlookers believed the *Titanic* to be a technological masterpiece. Perhaps the *Titanic* was even unsinkable. In 1912, anything seemed possible.

But the RMS *Titanic* never arrived at its final destination — and neither did more than two-thirds of the passengers and crew on board the ship. Had too much faith been placed in technology? Had the *Titanic*'s crew been overly confident of their vessel's size and strength?

This book focuses on the science of the *Titanic* and the ship's short life. You can visit the *Titanic* as it is assembled, piece by piece, in the dockyard, travel with it out to sea, and watch as it founders and sinks. Then, you can discover it on the ocean floor and explore possible explanations for some of the unsolved mysteries of the *Titanic*.

The Largest and Finest Steamers in the world

"OLYMPIC" 882½ FEET LONG

WHITE STAR LINE

45,000 TONS REGISTER

"TITANIC" 92½ FEET BROAD

[Top] *The biggest ship ever built was big news. One way to share in the excitement was to send postcards such as these, produced before the ship was even launched.* [Bottom] *Illustration from White Star Line brochure.*

WHAT'S IN A NAME?

The full name of the *Titanic* was RMS *Titanic*. RMS stood for "Royal Mail Steamer," and a ship with this prefix to its name carried the mail of Great Britain. On its maiden voyage, the *Titanic* was carrying 3,500 bags of mail, all of which went down with the ship. The word "titanic" means "of great size" — an accurate description of the largest ship of its day! But it also means "like the Titans." In Greek mythology, the Titans were a race of giants. Strong and daring, they were nevertheless defeated and succeeded by the Olympian gods, led by Zeus. Those who named the *Titanic* could never have imagined that, like the Titans, the ship was doomed to vanish from the face of the Earth.

CROSSING THE ATLANTIC

Before engines were invented, sailing ships were the only way to cross an ocean. Because these wooden-hulled vessels relied on the power of the wind, the length of a typical voyage was unpredictable. It could take a few weeks — or a few months. In addition, the living quarters were cramped and often uncomfortable.

The first real steam engine was built in 1712, and a greatly improved version was developed in 1769. This machine would change ocean travel forever. Experiments with boats powered by steam engines began in the late 1700s. Coal was used to heat water in boilers and produce steam, just as water heated in a teakettle does. The energy from the steam was used to power pistons, and the pistons turned paddle wheels that moved the ship.

During the 1830s, paddle-wheel steamships were used regularly to cross the Atlantic. The trip could take between two to four weeks. In the 1840s, propellers replaced paddle wheels on ocean-going vessels. Wooden hulls were replaced by stronger and heavier iron hulls better able to withstand the constant vibration of the steam engines. But sailing ships were still used on long voyages. Wind was free, and sailing ships never needed to refuel.

More powerful piston engines, such as reciprocating and triple expansion engines, were invented after 1870. Ships with these engines could travel farther without needing to recoal. Steamships finally took over from sailing ships on most long-distance routes.

By 1875, the fastest ships could cross the ocean in 7 1/2 days, although most steamships took about 10 to 14 days. A speedy trip cost more than a longer trip on a slower boat, but many passengers

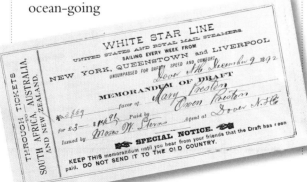

White Star Line transatlantic ticket from 1892

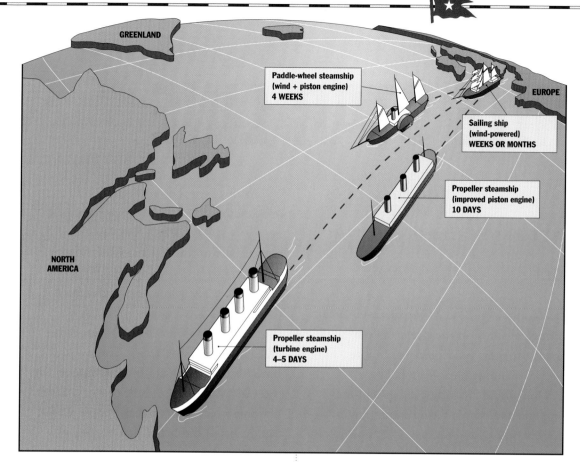

GREENLAND

EUROPE

NORTH AMERICA

Paddle-wheel steamship
(wind + piston engine)
4 WEEKS

Sailing ship
(wind-powered)
WEEKS OR MONTHS

Propeller steamship
(improved piston engine)
10 DAYS

Propeller steamship
(turbine engine)
4–5 DAYS

When a sailing ship left on a transatlantic voyage during the 1800s, the passengers never knew if they would be weeks or months at sea. With paddle-wheel steamships, which used coal as a source of steam power, trips became more predictable. Passengers could count on crossing the Atlantic within 15 days to one month. Propellers and the new engines that turned them made possible a transatlantic voyage of only about 10 days. By the early 1900s, the turbine engine had cut this time in half.

were willing to pay for extra speed. The more powerful ships were also bigger ships, allowing extra room for much cheaper accommodation on the lower decks. A third-class ticket guaranteed little more than a bed, but with the transatlantic trip taking less than two weeks, passengers on a tight budget could carry enough of their own food and bedding to last the journey.

By 1900, steel — lighter and more flexible than iron and bendable into any shape — was replacing iron in shipbuilding.

UP IN THE AIR

Today, if you want to cross the Atlantic Ocean, you can hop onto an airplane and reach your destination in several hours. A hundred years ago, air travel was unknown. The Wright brothers didn't successfully fly the first powered airplane until 1908 — and that flight lasted only 12 seconds! It wasn't until the mid-1930s that travelers were willing to risk the uncertainties of this new mode of transportation to cross a wide ocean. And it wasn't until 1957 that planes outstripped ships as the most popular way to cross the Atlantic.

THE WHITE STAR LINE

The 1900s began the age of the great Atlantic passenger liners. Now, when you wished to cross the ocean, you could choose from among hundreds of ships from many major lines. Competition for your cash was fierce — and so was competition to provide the fastest transatlantic vessel. Britain's Cunard Line had introduced two express liners in 1907. These ships — the *Lusitania* and the *Mauretania* — could cross the Atlantic in just four and a half days, thanks to an even newer, more powerful type of engine — the steam turbine. The efficient steam turbine engine still used coal to create steam, but it did not use pistons. Instead, much as wind pushes the blades on a pinwheel, the steam pressure rotated blades that turned the propellers directly.

The *Lusitania* and the *Mauretania* were also the biggest ships on the ocean, able to pack aboard the most passengers. And more passengers meant greater profit.

How could any other steamship line compete? Only by offering something different, something unique. The American-owned White Star Line decided to offer comfort. They would build three luxury ocean liners offering all the comforts of home — and more. White Star's new ships would provide better facilities for passengers — from first-class to third-class — than any other liner. They would also be big. Huge, in fact.

At this time, before homes had radios or televisions, a great many people read newspapers. The White Star Line used newspapers on both sides of the Atlantic for their advertising campaign. Their extravagant advertisements highlighted the modern conveniences and safety features of the ships. "The Queen of the Ocean: *Titanic*…the Latest, Largest, and Finest Steamer Afloat," boasted one ad. In the early years of the 20th century, words like these had great appeal. People were caught up in the belief that biggest was best. Who could resist this chance of a lifetime — to be pampered on the biggest ship ever built, an island-sized structure powered and maintained by the most advanced technology of the time?

The White Star Line hired Harland and Wolff, shipbuilders located in Belfast,

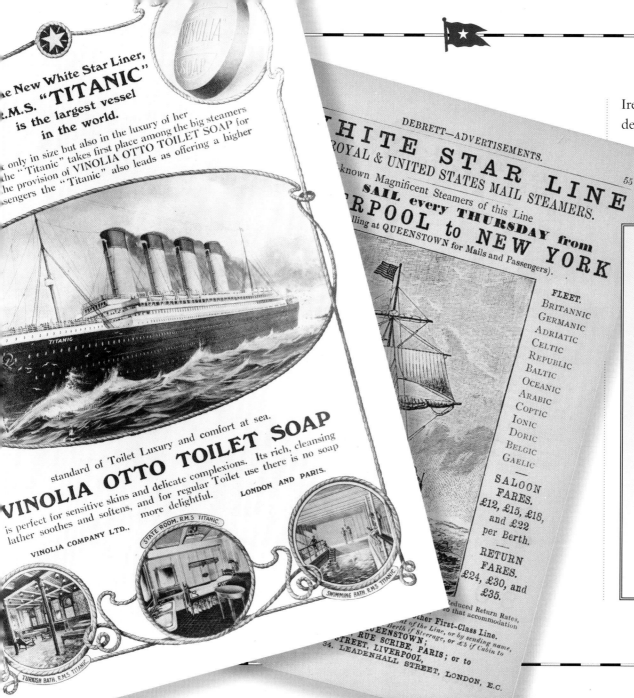

Ireland, to build the three giant ships. They decided to name the vessels the *Olympic*, the *Titanic*, and the *Gigantic*.

EMIGRANT SHIPS

I n the early 1900s, a growing number of people were leaving Europe to settle in North America. Most of these emigrants traveled third-class, sharing cooking facilities, washrooms, and dormitories located on the lower decks of the ships. The bigger a ship was, the more room it had available on its lower decks. To meet the new demand for third-class accommodation, steamship lines began building their ships larger and larger. Many of these big passenger ships, including the *Titanic*, were legally classified as "emigrant ships."

For the biggest ship in the world, the biggest gantry in the world had to be built. It covered two huge slipways — one for the Titanic and one for its sister ship, the Olympic. [Inset] The shipyard men leave work.

BUILDING THE TITANIC

Harland and Wolff had a problem. Until now, their shipyard had never built a ship as large as the *Titanic*. Ships were built on sloping slipways located at the water's edge. When a new ship was launched, it slid down the slipway, usually stern first, and floated in the water. In order to build the three huge ships ordered by the White Star Line, Harland and Wolff had to demolish three of their slipways and build two much larger ones, spanned by a giant gantry.

A gantry is a towerlike metal framework along which cranes move, carrying ship's parts and machinery from one end of the growing vessel to the other. The gantry covering the two enormous new slipways was the biggest in the world, spanning an area almost one and a half times the size of a football field and reaching as high as a 19-story building. On the slips under this gantry, the *Olympic* and then the *Titanic* would begin to take shape. First, however, hundreds of blueprints and drawings were created for the builders to refer to as the ship was being built.

Construction of the *Titanic* began in the slipway on March 31, 1909. Ships are built from the bottom up, so the first part of the *Titanic* to be built was the keel. The keel is the backbone of a ship — a continuous line of steel plates running the whole length of the vessel. Once the *Titanic*'s keel was laid down on the slipway, it was time to construct the double bottom hull.

The tank top — the bottom-most deck — will have to support the weight of the Titanic's three massive engines and 29 gigantic boilers. Here, the tank top is being laid over the ship's double bottom hull and keel.

It took almost a year to build the frames — or ribs — of the ship. The rising frames dwarf the men below as they prepare to install the stern post and rudder port.

Most shipbuilders of the *Titanic*'s day thought that the bottom of a ship needed the greatest protection, because they believed that accidents were most likely to occur from collisions with underwater objects. Thus, like many large passenger steamers of the time, the *Titanic* was built with a double bottom hull — an outer shell and an inner shell — that extended along the bottom of the ship to the sides. The plates on the inner shell were slightly thinner than those on the outer shell. A double bottom hull was thought to provide extra safety. If the outer hull was damaged or pierced, the inner shell would likely remain intact. Any water coming through the outer hull would thus be contained and not spread to other areas of the ship.

Now the ship was ready to be framed. The frames are the ribs of a ship. They are attached to the keel. The frames on the *Titanic* were between 2 feet (0.6 m) and 3 feet (almost 1 m) apart. They formed a U-shape, at the top of which the upper decks of the ship would eventually be built. The huge horizontal deck beams would be attached to the frames to support the decks. The *Titanic* would have 10 steel decks in total.

Upright pieces of metal, called the stern post and the stem, were then installed. The stem was attached to the bow (the front) of the *Titanic*, and the stern post was attached to the stern (the rear) of the ship, in line with the keel. The *Titanic*'s sides would later be joined to these two posts for support. Together with the keel, the stem and the stern post formed the ship's strongest structure. The framing of the *Titanic* took about a year and was completed on April 6, 1910.

Next, the *Titanic*'s plates were prepared.

Sheets of steel were cut to size and then shaped either flat or curved depending on where they were to be placed. These plates were used to form the hull, or outer shell of the ship, and the decks. The plates on the outer shell and some deck plates were 1 inch (2.5 cm) thick. Other deck plates were 1 1/2 inches (almost 4 cm) thick.

Thousands of steel plates were needed to form the *Titanic*'s hull. The plates were positioned side by side, with the edges overlapping. The overlapping portions were then fastened to the frames and to each other with 4-inch (10 cm) wrought-iron rivets. These rivets were mushroom-shaped, with a bulging head attached to a narrower stem. Workers heated the rivets for three or four minutes until they were red hot. Rows of holes had already been made where the hull plates overlapped. Into each of these holes, a hot rivet was inserted, with its head pressing firmly against the plate and its stem sticking out on the opposite side. The rivet was held steady while a worker used a hammer or hydraulic riveter to press flat the protruding hot metal of the stem. This

secured the rivet in place.

More than three million rivets were used on the huge ocean liner. Half a million rivets, weighing a total of 270 tons (245 t), were used on the bottom of the hull alone, to give it extra strength. In some places on the bottom plating, double or even quadruple rows of rivets were used to hold together the hull plates. The riveting was a massive job.

The *Titanic*'s plating was completed by October 19, 1910, but there was much more structural work to be done. For example, steel walls, called bulkheads, were constructed to divide the *Titanic* into 16 compartments. Each bulkhead ran from one side of the ship to the other. Bulkheads were placed at intervals along the entire length of the ship. The bulkheads were watertight, but passengers and crew would be able to

It takes six months, hundreds of workers, thousands of steel plates, and more than three million iron rivets to build the Titanic's hull.

[Left] *The launch: After a cry of "Stand clear!" the hull slips down a long, sloping, greased platform into the water for the first time.* [Below] *At the fitting-out dock, a giant floating crane installs engines and boilers.*

move between the compartments through watertight doors. In an emergency, such as a puncture in the hull, the flick of an electric switch located on the bridge would instantly close and seal the doors, preventing water from moving from compartment to compartment. According to a leading engineering journal of the day, this system made the *Titanic* "practically unsinkable."

On May 31, 1911, more than two years after the keel had been laid, the hull of the *Titanic* was ready to be launched. Although it had been painted for the occasion, the hull was still an empty shell. The ship was not yet fitted with masts, funnels, or upper deck structures, electrical or mechanical items — such as wiring, pipework, pumps, and motors — or the

features that would make it comfortable for passengers: carpets, beds, tables, chairs, gym equipment, and decorations.

But this didn't matter to the 100,000 excited people who gathered to see the launch. Even as a bare shell, the hull was impressive. It was the *Titanic*'s incredible size, after all, that had most sparked the public's imagination and caused engineering and scientific journals to rave about the ship. A cheer went up as the 883-foot (269 m) *Titanic* glided gracefully into the water of River Lagan. The ship was about four city blocks long — the largest moving object yet made by human beings!

The ship was towed to the fitting-out dock where *Titanic*'s heavy electrical equipment, its three engines, and its 29 boilers would be installed. Normally, this would have been done at the shipyard's engine-works dock. But the *Titanic* was simply too big to fit! Instead, the heavy machinery had to come to the ship. It was installed by a 200-ton (180 t) floating crane, one of the largest floating cranes in the world at the time.

ELECTRICITY = SAFETY?

The *Titanic* was equipped with the most up-to-date electrical technology available. Everyone believed this made it an extremely safe vessel. The ship carried four main generating engines, plus two additional auxiliary engines for emergency use. The generating engines provided electricity for more than 150 different motors on board the ship. Electricity powered everything from the lights, potato-peelers, electric irons, and electric baths to the deck cranes, machine-shop tools, loudspeakers, and fans.

Communication within the ship was improved by electricity. Electricity powered the telephone that connected the crow's-nest to the bridge. The telephone reduced the time needed to receive and execute an emergency order to change the ship's course or alter its speed.

Electricity also powered the ship's wireless radio system. Instead of using telegraph wires to carry messages, the new wireless system used invisible radio waves. In 1901, Guglielmo Marconi had sent radio signals across the Atlantic for the first time, using the radio system he invented. By 1912, most passenger vessels had wireless

technology aboard. Wireless operators sent messages using Morse code, a system of dashes and dots representing the letters of the alphabet.

On the *Titanic*, wireless signals were transmitted using the ship's antenna. Due to the antenna's great height and the amount of power the ship's generators could supply, the *Titanic*'s radio was more powerful than most shipboard radios. Under perfect conditions, it could transmit more than 500 miles (805 km).

The *Titanic*'s two wireless operators worked in shifts. They relayed messages for passengers and, more important, communicated with the shore and other ships — to send and receive messages, warnings, and navigational information. If this information was received and passed on to the ship's officers promptly, it could greatly increase the ship's safety.

But in 1912, ships were not required by law to keep their wireless operating 24 hours a day. If the *Californian,* a ship roughly 14 miles away from the *Titanic* on the night of April 14, had had its radio on that night, it would have heard the *Titanic*'s distress calls. Disaster might have been averted.

A ship's wireless operators were responsible for sending and receiving all messages.

Over the next 10 months, millions of man-hours went into preparing the great ship for passengers. Miles and miles of pipes and electrical wiring were put in place. Designers had prepared detailed drawings of the dining rooms, restaurants, staterooms, and other interior areas. Now, the walls and floors of these rooms, and the staircases between decks, were being built.

On February 3, 1912, the *Titanic* was floated from the fitting-out dock into the dry dock. The water was then pumped out of the dry dock so that workers could get at the bottom of the ship. They installed the three propellers and gave another coat of paint to the hull. Then the *Titanic* was refloated and returned to the fitting-out dock.

By mid-February, the funnels and masts had been erected, the ship's lifeboats were in place, the tiles for the swimming pool were being laid, and the first- and second-class elevators were being installed.

In March, floors were polished while furniture was piled up, ready to be put in place. The ship's compasses, life preservers, and security safes — and the 21-light candelabra for the main staircase — arrived.

By April, the *Titanic* was finally ready for its first voyage. What a magnificent vessel! It was luxurious in its furnishings, as tall from keel to bridge as a 13-story building, and, at 46,328 tons (42 020 t), bigger than any other ship in the world.

Was the great ship unsinkable? Neither the shipbuilders, Harland and Wolff, nor the owners, the White Star Line, ever claimed that it was. They didn't need to! The world had watched, awestruck, as the *Titanic* grew…and grew…and grew. Who could imagine anything powerful enough to damage a ship that size?

It is March, 1912. Back at the fitting-out dock, the Titanic *[at right] is being outfitted. The funnels and masts are now on, and the ship's interior is being readied. Beside the* Titanic, *the* Olympic *is getting a propeller blade replaced.*

TITANIC FACTS

1 Length: 882.6 feet (269 m)
Height (from keel to tops of funnels): 175 feet (55 m)
Weight: 46,328 tons (42 020 t)
Top speed: 23–24 knots

2 The *Titanic* could carry 2,603 passengers and 944 crew. About nine of today's Boeing 747 jumbo jets would be needed to carry the same number of people.

3 The *Titanic*'s passenger accommodation was split into three classes. A first-class suite cost as much as £870 (about US$50,000 in today's dollars) — one way. A second-class berth cost £12. A one-way, third-class ticket cost £3 to £8 — a month's wages for most workers in 1912.

4 The *Titanic* was the first ship to have a gymnasium and a swimming pool. First- and second-class passengers could play squash or go to a concert, relax in the library or play cards in the smoking room, bath in one of the electric baths or ride the elevator up to the top deck to enjoy the view and walk in the fresh ocean air.

Eight hired musicians entertained passengers. First-class passengers could exercise on the equipment in the gymnasium.

5 There were more specialist lookouts on the *Titanic* — six in all, two per shift — than on any other ship on the ocean in 1912.

6 The *Titanic* was almost identical to her slightly smaller sister-ship, the *Olympic*. When the *Olympic* was launched, three months before the *Titanic*, it was the largest ship in the world. In fact, the *Olympic* was launched with more fanfare and excitement than the *Titanic*. It was only after the terrible disaster of the *Titanic*'s sinking that the *Titanic* surpassed the *Olympic* in the public's imagination. The *Olympic* was withdrawn from service in 1935, after making 257 round-trip crossings of the Atlantic Ocean.

Built in 1913, the *Titanic*'s other sister-ship, the *Gigantic*, never saw service as an ocean liner. Re-named the *Britannic*, it was commissioned as a hospital ship in World War II. In 1916, the *Britannic* hit a mine in the Aegean Sea and sank.

7 Today, the world's largest cruise ship is the *Voyager of the Seas*, which is 137.4 feet (42 m) longer than the *Titanic*. The *Voyager of the Seas* carries 3,114 passengers and 1,100 crew.

THE TURN OF THE PROPELLERS

The *Titanic's* propellers first turned on April 2, 1912. What force could move the largest ship ever built? The power of pressurized steam. The steam was produced in massive boilers 15 to 17 feet (4.6–5.2 m) high and weighed nearly 100 tons (90 t).

The *Titanic's* two reciprocating steam engines were the largest engines that had ever been built. Each was more than 30 feet (9 m) high, and each powered one three-bladed propeller, which measured 23 feet (7 m) across. One of these propellers was located on each side of the ship. The low-pressure steam turbine engine powered the four-bladed center propeller, which measured 16 feet (5 m) across.

1 Night and day, stokers shoveled coal into the ship's 149 furnaces.

2 The coal burned and heated the water in the ship's 29 boilers, creating steam.

3 The steam from the boilers traveled through steel pipes to the engines.

4 Smoke and waste gases from the coal burning in the furnaces traveled from the boilers through other pipes to the ship's three working funnels, or smokestacks. The ship's fourth funnel was used for ventilation.

5 The steam traveled through a series of four different cylinders — enclosed cylindrical chambers — in each reciprocating engine. The pressure of the steam inside the cylinder set a piston — a metal disk fitting closely within the cylinder — in motion, up and down.

6 The pistons were each attached to a rod and a crank. The four moving cranks connected to each reciprocating engine worked together, taking the forward force exerted by the pistons and redirecting it to rotate a 2-foot-(0.6 m) wide propeller shaft that turned one of the ship's two side propellers. The side propellers could move the ship forward and backward.

7 The turbine engine made use of the steam that was left over after passing through the reciprocating engine cylinders. In the turbine engine, the flow of steam turned angled blades set in a rotor, a revolving, wheel-like device.

8 The rotor was attached to a propeller shaft. As the rotor blades turned, the shaft turned, rotating the *Titanic's* center propeller. The turbine could only operate to move the ship forward.

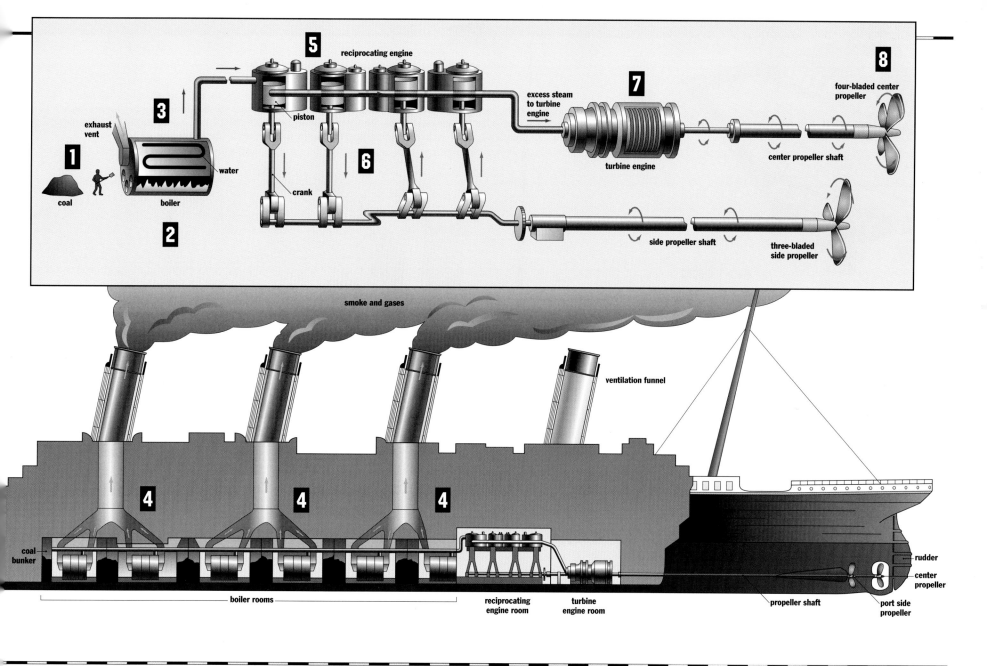

5 reciprocating engine

8 four-bladed center propeller

7

excess steam to turbine engine

piston

3

6

turbine engine

center propeller shaft

water

1

boiler

crank

2

side propeller shaft

three-bladed side propeller

coal

exhaust vent

smoke and gases

ventilation funnel

4

4

4

coal bunker

rudder

center propeller

boiler rooms

reciprocating engine room

turbine engine room

propeller shaft

port side propeller

At 6:00 A.M. on April 2, five tugboats escorted the Titanic out of the fitting-out basin. The tugs cast off, and the ship was unfettered in the water for the first time. The Titanic's boiler steam was directed to the reciprocating engines and from there to the turbine engine. The ship was alive! All day, the Titanic underwent sea trials. By 8:00 P.M., the ship had passed all its tests. It was steaming to England — on its first night at sea. [Left and facing page] White Star Line luggage stickers

WHITE STAR LINE

ROOM

VIA

NAME

BOOKED TO

SAILING

STEAMER

FULL FOREIGN ADDRESS

WANTED

FIRST CLASS

AWAY

On April 2, 1912, the *Titanic* left the Harland and Wolff dockyards and headed down the Irish Sea to Southampton, England. The ship arrived on April 3 and remained for one week. During this time, final preparations were made, such as loading hundreds of bags of mail and huge quantities of food and drink onto the ship.

On April 10, the crew and more than 1,500 passengers came aboard. Shortly after noon that day, crowds of onlookers watched as the *Titanic* was maneuvered away from its dock by six tugboats.

But the transatlantic journey had yet to begin. First, the *Titanic* had to cross the English Channel to Cherbourg, France, and then return across the Channel to Queenstown (Cohb), Ireland, to pick up hundreds of passengers and hundreds more bags of mail.

By the afternoon of Thursday, April 11, all the passengers and crew — 2,228 people in all — were aboard. Passengers waved farewell to friends and family as the *Titanic* left the harbor. Hours later, as the sun began to set, the *Titanic* steamed past Ireland's southern shore. Like a glittering palace — a small, bright, moving island — the ship headed out on its maiden voyage across the Atlantic Ocean.

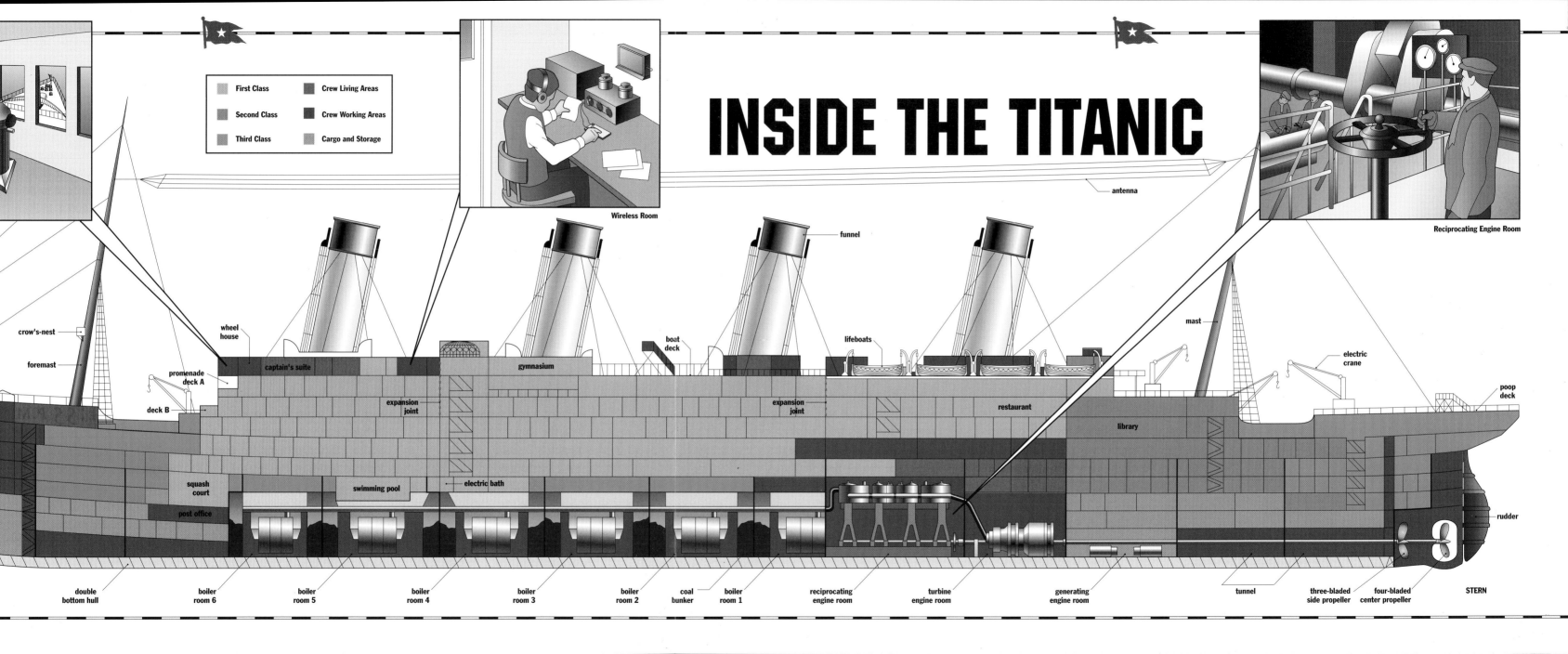

INSIDE THE TITANIC

Wireless Room

Reciprocating Engine Room

antenna

funnel

crow's-nest

wheel house

mast

electric crane

foremast

captain's suite

boat deck

lifeboats

promenade deck A

gymnasium

expansion joint

expansion joint

restaurant

poop deck

deck B

library

squash court

swimming pool

electric bath

rudder

post office

double bottom hull

boiler room 6

boiler room 5

boiler room 4

boiler room 3

boiler room 2

coal bunker

boiler room 1

reciprocating engine room

turbine engine room

generating engine room

tunnel

three-bladed side propeller

four-bladed center propeller

STERN

Legend:
- First Class
- Second Class
- Third Class
- Crew Living Areas
- Crew Working Areas
- Cargo and Storage

FINAL HOURS

The *Titanic* has been at sea for three days. Its first transatlantic voyage is almost over. Soon the ship will pass Newfoundland and draw close to the mainland of North America. It is late on the night of April 14. The iceberg, rising like a massive wall out of the water, is suddenly, frighteningly, blocking the way.

On the bridge, Sixth Officer James Moody answers Lookout Frederick Fleet's telephone call from the crow's-nest and repeats Fleet's words to First Officer William Murdoch: "Iceberg right ahead!"

Immediately Murdoch reacts. He decides to halt the forward movement of the ship, which is traveling at 22 to 23 knots,

Sixth Officer James Moody [left] and First Officer William Murdoch [right] were on the bridge when the Titanic hit the iceberg.

only 1 or 2 knots below full speed. (The speed of a ship is described in knots. One knot is one nautical mile — about 2,025 yards [1853 m] — per hour.) Murdoch rushes to the telegraph used to signal the engine room from the bridge and orders that the engines be stopped and then reversed. A split second later, Murdoch makes what is perhaps a fatal decision — to turn the ship and try to avoid hitting the iceberg. Murdoch orders Quartermaster Robert Hichens, who is steering the ship, to spin the wheel "hard over" — until it can turn no more.

Then, Murdoch prepares for the worst — a collision that might allow seawater to enter the ship. He rings the alarm bells for 10 seconds in all the engine-room compartments, warning the engine-room crew to get out. He flips the switch

Crew members could climb ladders to escape compartments when the watertight doors closed.

that will electronically close the engine rooms' watertight doors so that incoming water will not flow through the doors from one compartment to another.

The *Titanic* is still heading toward the iceberg. Can the ship possibly avoid a collision? From the crow's-nest, the lookouts watch, holding their breath. Slowly, slowly, the huge ship begins to turn left, and for a moment, it looks as if it will escape harm.

About half a minute after the ship starts to turn, Fleet and Lee and others aboard the ship feel a shudder. The *Titanic* has rubbed alongside a submerged portion of the iceberg. Far beneath the water-line, the ship's 1-inch- (2.5 cm) thick steel side splits open.

Captain Edward Smith has been sleeping soundly in his

Captain Edward Smith stopped the ship.

berth. Alerted to the collision, he hurries immediately to the bridge. Perhaps wishing to check for damage to the propellers or rudder, Smith orders the halted engines to be set at half ahead, resuming the ship's forward movement. Within moments, however, he decides that all forward motion should be stopped. This will reduce the speed at which any seawater will flood into the ship. The three main engines are stopped. As the *Titanic's* propellers cease spinning, never to run again, the ship continues on in the curve it had begun to avoid the iceberg. Then, it begins to drift, carried along by the Atlantic's slow southerly current.

Captain Smith orders the ship's carpenter to sound the ship for damage. Thomas Andrews,

Thomas Andrews realised right away that the ship was doomed.

the managing director of Harland and Wolff's design department, conducts his own inspection. It does not look good. Just 10 minutes after the collision, the water in the bow has risen 14 feet (4.3 m) above the keel.

Fifteen minutes after the collision, the post office on lower Deck G — one level above the boiler rooms — is flooding. Andrews, who had full responsibility for the design

THE ICE WAS NO SURPRISE

T he *Titanic*'s wireless operators had been informed by other ships' wireless operators of sightings of ice in the area. They passed on several of these warnings — indicating ice to the north of the ship — to the officers on the bridge. As a result, on the morning of April 12, Captain Smith altered the *Titanic*'s route to a more southerly course to try and avoid the ice. But he maintained his ship's speed. According to some *Titanic* historians, Captain Smith reacted to the ice warnings just as other ship captains of the time likely would have. Before the *Titanic* disaster, most ship captains believed that if an iceberg could be spotted, it could be avoided — even if a ship was moving quickly. Some historians also think that, had the *Titanic*'s new communications technology been used properly, the ship's collision with the iceberg could have been prevented. Wireless was still a fairly new technology aboard ships, and there was not yet any standard procedure for making sure all "ship's business" messages reached the bridge. Tragically, because the wireless operators were very busy sending and receiving passengers' messages, there were ice warnings that the captain never received. Common sense should have told the operators that ice warnings were more important than passengers' messages, yet not all warnings were recorded and relayed. At 10:55 P.M. on April 14, a critical wireless message warned of an enormous ice field, 78 miles (126 km) long, directly in the *Titanic*'s path. This message — and another like it, received a few hours earlier — was never passed on to the captain or the officers. Disaster resulted.

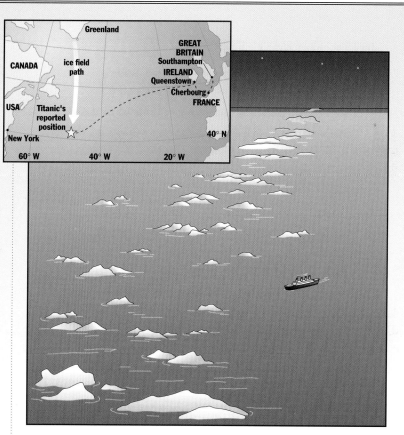

To ships in the Titanic's *day, the many icebergs that travel south near the east coast of Newfoundland during the spring months represented one of the chief dangers in crossing the Atlantic.* [Inset] *The star marks where the* Titanic *and the iceberg collided.*

WHY DIDN'T THE LOOKOUTS SEE THE ICEBERG SOONER?

The iceberg that doomed the *Titanic* began its life far north of where the *Titanic* sank, as part of the ice cap that covers Greenland. This very thick ice cap is actually a slow-moving glacier, which is continually pushing its tip into the sea. Warm spring weather causes chunks of rock-hard ice to break off, or "calve," from the glacier's tip, becoming icebergs.

Icebergs can be milky white or glacial blue. They can also be black or brown in areas where the ice has scraped across rock, or even green, if seaweed and other marine plants become attached. They can be as small as a piano or rise as high above the water as a 15-story building. An iceberg floats with six-sevenths of its mass below the sea surface, so only a small amount of the whole iceberg is visible above the water. Most icebergs melt within about two years.

The iceberg that the *Titanic* eventually hit had drifted south from Western Greenland to near the island of Newfoundland, off the east coast of Canada. From there, it was carried by ocean currents into the transatlantic shipping route where the *Titanic* was sailing on April 14, 1912.

Why didn't the *Titanic*'s lookouts see this iceberg in time to avoid a collision with it? They had been put on the alert for icebergs, and the sky had been clear that night. When Captain Smith retired for the evening, he commented that if there was even the slightest bit of haze the ship would have to slow down. Traveling fast would be too dangerous if they could not see well ahead. The captain asked the crew to wake him if there was any doubt about what to do. Because Captain Smith wasn't roused, most *Titanic* historians think that the night remained clear right up to the collision.

But a clear sky did not ensure that icebergs would be easy to spot. In fact, the lookouts were working under difficult conditions that night. The sea was calm, which meant there were no waves to wash up against an iceberg and make it more visible. There was no moon and thus no light to reflect off an iceberg's surface. The iceberg that loomed out of the darkness may have overturned within the last hour. An overturned iceberg loses its shiny surface and reflects little light, making it invisible to the eye. Under such conditions, almost any iceberg would have been impossible to see against the night sky — until it was too late.

The iceberg that sank the Titanic *rose around 60 feet (18 m) above the water. Six-sevenths of the iceberg — another 360 feet (108 m) — lay hidden below the water.*

1/7
2/7
3/7
4/7
5/7
6/7
7/7

12:00 P.M.

An alarm bell summons all not-on-duty engineers to join those already on duty in the engine rooms in the bottom of the ship. The engineering crew begin pumping water out of the flooded compartments, trying to shore up the bulkheads against leaking and collapse.

The 29 boilers that provided steam to the ship's main engines are still red hot. The engineers shut down most of the boilers, to prevent them exploding like bombs when they contact the freezing seawater. But they can't shut down all of them. Some of the boilers must remain working to provide steam to power at

SOS

Since the first years of the 1900s, when the use of Morse code by ships had begun, the international maritime distress call had been CQD. CQD meant "Pay attention. There is an important message to follow." But in 1908, this alert signal was changed to SOS. SOS did not stand for any particular words, such as "Save Our Ship." It was chosen because the signal — three dots (S), three dashes (O), three dots (S) — was easy to send and receive and was unlikely to be confused with any other call. Was the *Titanic*'s call for help in 1912 the first SOS distress call ever sent out, as some claim? The *Titanic*'s wireless operators had been fortunate enough never to have faced an emergency before, so it was certainly the first SOS that *they* ever radioed. But the very first recorded SOS was sent in 1908 by another White Star liner, the *Republic*, after it collided with the *Florida*.

Wireless messages sent by the Titanic's operators tell of the worsening situation aboard. (M.G.Y. are the call letters assigned to the Titanic.)

least one or two of the ship's four generators. These are providing electricity to the ship's lights, wireless system, and pumps. The engineering crew work desperately to keep the generators dry.

12:05 A.M.

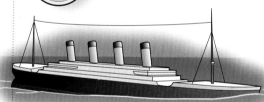

Captain Smith orders the crew to uncover the lifeboats. Water is now sloshing across the floor of the squash court, 32 feet (10 m) above the keel, and pouring into the sixth watertight compartment, Boiler Room No. 5.

Captain Smith goes to the wireless room and orders John Phillips, the chief wireless operator, to call for help.

Huge quantities of steam have been accumulating in the shut-down boilers. It must be released to reduce pressure, otherwise the boilers will explode. The engineers divert the steam up the funnels, and the hiss and bellow created is deafening to those on deck.

There were 3,560 life jackets and 48 life preservers aboard the Titanic — enough for everyone, but of little use in the freezing Atlantic waters.

The order is given to load the lifeboats. Passengers are putting on life jackets. Because the ship is beginning to tilt at a severe angle, the elevators are no longer working, and passengers must climb the stairs to reach the boat deck. Some are convinced to head for the lifeboats. The lifeboat drill scheduled for earlier on the voyage had been canceled, and the crew have not been assigned to specific boat stations. They organize themselves as best they can and try to prepare the boats for lowering.

12:45 A.M.

The first lifeboat is lowered, slightly less than half full. Many of the other lifeboats to leave

After entering the lifeboats, the Titanic's passengers would spend from two to six hours on the open sea before being taken aboard the Carpathia. [Right] White Star Line officer's whistle

the Titanic aren't full either. Large numbers of third-class passengers remain below deck. Some are unaware of the danger, while others are having difficulty getting to the boat deck. Many of the passengers on deck still do not want to believe the Titanic is sinking, even though there is now a noticeable tilt in the bow.

From the deck of the enormous ship, staying aboard seems safer than getting into one of the tiny boats and being lowered into the dark and freezing water far below.

Distress rockets are fired from the bridge at seven-minute intervals for about one hour. Seeing these, many passengers

WATERTIGHT SHIP?

How, after his early inspection of the damage, was ship designer Thomas Andrews so sure that the *Titanic* was doomed? Only part of the ship was flooding. Wasn't there a chance it could stay afloat until help arrived?

Andrews' inspection had revealed that the ship was damaged on its side, below the waterline. If the damage had been to the bottom of the ship, the double bottom hull might have been able to contain the water. But the *Titanic* had hit the iceberg well above the double bottom hull, and the water was pouring directly into the ship.

Although separated by steel walls, called bulkheads, none of the 16 compartments of the *Titanic* was really watertight. Most of the compartment sides reached only as high as Deck E (two decks above the waterline), and none were sealed on top. If only two or three — maybe even four — compartments had been flooded, this would not have been a problem. The weight of two or three compartments filled with water would not have sunk the ship or tilted it enough to cause water to spill over into an adjoining compartment.

But when the *Titanic* was damaged by the iceberg, about 12 feet (3.6 m) above its keel, 5 of the 16 compartments immediately began to flood, and the ship was doomed. The bow of the ship quickly began to sink with the weight of all the water. The water flooding the five compartments at the bow of the ship rose until it spilled over the top of the fifth compartment and into the one behind it. Andrews knew that the flooding of the ship could not be stopped. From the sixth compartment, the water would pour into the seventh, and so on. The end result? The weight of all this water would sink the "practically unsinkable" *Titanic*.

The Titanic*'s 16 compartments had watertight bulkheads, but they were open on top — like an ice-cube tray. Water spilled from the damaged compartments into the intact ones, pulling the ship under.*

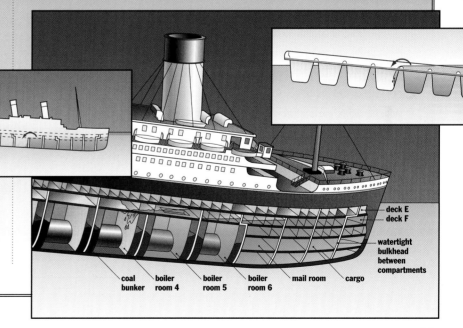

deck E
deck F

watertight bulkhead between compartments

coal bunker · boiler room 4 · boiler room 5 · boiler room 6 · mail room · cargo

STEERING THE TITANIC

By the time the lookouts spotted the iceberg, it was about 500 yards (460 m) away, less than two lengths of the *Titanic*. At that point, it was impossible for the ship, moving at the speed it was, to stop before striking the iceberg. But why couldn't the ship turn out of the way in time? The answer lies in the workings of a ship.

The *Titanic* was steered with its main wheel, located in the wheelhouse behind the bridge. The main wheel was connected to the ship's massive rudder — as tall as a 10-story building and weighing 100 tons (90 t). The position of the rudder determined the direction in which the ship traveled.

For a ship to be able to turn, it needs to be moving. If the ship's rudder is positioned straight back, or "amidships," water flows past the rudder, and the ship sails straight ahead. When the rudder is turned to either side, the water presses against it. This turns the ship.

When the lookouts reported the iceberg, First Officer Murdoch immediately ordered the engines stopped, then reversed. But, of the *Titanic*'s three propellers, only the two side propellers, powered by the reciprocating engines, could be put into reverse. The turbine engine and the center propeller — which was directly in line with the rudder — remained stopped. This meant that there was no longer nearly as much water flowing over the ship's rudder.

The faster a ship is moving, the greater the pressure of the water against the rudder, and the faster the ship can turn. When a ship is slowing down — as the *Titanic* was when Murdoch ordered the engines reversed — the flow of water across the rudder is reduced, and the ship cannot turn as quickly. Some experts believe that if the ship's engines had been left running full ahead during the turn the *Titanic* could have turned more quickly — and perhaps avoided the iceberg.

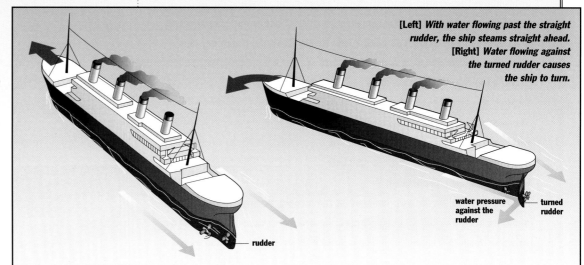

[Left] *With water flowing past the straight rudder, the ship steams straight ahead.*
[Right] *Water flowing against the turned rudder causes the ship to turn.*

water pressure against the rudder

turned rudder

rudder

are now persuaded that the ship is actually in serious trouble and there is cause for alarm.

Since hitting the iceberg, the sinking *Titanic*, with engines stopped, is carried slowly along by the ocean's southerly current.

1:40 A.M.

Some of the remaining lifeboats are more fully loaded. It is now clear that there are not nearly enough lifeboats for everyone. The danger of remaining on the *Titanic* is becoming more obvious. Some of the passengers begin to panic. "Women and children first," urge the crew. Some passengers act heroically and give up their seats to others. As the ship's

bow sinks deeper, the stern rises, and it becomes more and more difficult to lower the lifeboats.

In the bowels of the ship, brave engineers are still working in two boiler rooms to maintain power to supply electricity to the pumps, lights, and wireless.

2:05 A.M.

Hundreds of people watch from the decks as the last lifeboats are lowered. The entire bow of the *Titanic* is underwater. Many of the remaining 1,500 passengers head toward the stern of the ship, which is rising higher above the surface. The slippery deck is now at a

White Star Line officer's hat

steep incline. To keep from sliding into the ocean, people cling desperately to the railings and other fixed objects.

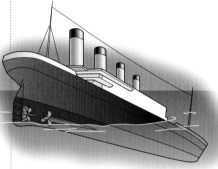

2:15 A.M.

The *Titanic* is at an even steeper angle. Suddenly, the ship lurches forward, and the three great propellers rise above the water.

The engineers remain at their stations below decks, still tending their dangerously tilting machinery. The wireless operators have been

calling for help for hours, even though their signal has been getting weaker. Captain Smith goes to the wireless room and advises the men that they may leave their posts. "It's every man for himself," he tells the crew. The bow of the *Titanic* plunges downward.

2:17 A.M.

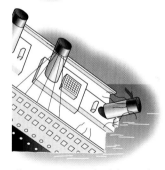

The guywires holding the forward funnel in place snap, and the funnel crashes forward. The *Titanic* sends out its last call for help.

LIFEBOAT MATH

The *Titanic* carried a total of 2,228 passengers and crew, yet the 16 lifeboats and 4 life rafts aboard provided room for only 1,178 people. To carry everyone on the ship, 16 more lifeboats and 1 more life raft would have been needed. If the *Titanic* had been carrying the 3,547 people it was certified to hold, 55 lifeboats would have been needed.

The Board of Trade regulations for emigrant ships had been set in 1884, almost three decades before the *Titanic* sailed. At that time, the largest emigrant ship afloat was *Lucania,* a steamer weighing in at just under 13,000 tons (11 800 t) — just over a quarter the size of the *Titanic.* The regulations lumped all ships of over 10,000 tons (9070 t) together, requiring them to carry a minimum of 16 lifeboats, with space for 550 people altogether.

If a ship carried more than 550 people, as did the *Titanic*, it was required to have enough lifeboats and life rafts for three-quarters more people than this, which is 412 people. Thus, the *Titanic*'s total legal requirement was 550 plus 412, or space for 962 people. With lifeboats and rafts capable of carrying 1,178 people, the *Titanic* was actually 216 spaces above the legal requirement.

Most ship owners believed that rescuing ships could respond to distress calls in plenty of time. They looked on lifeboats as simply a way to ferry people from a sinking vessel and assumed that it would take several trips to complete the job. No one ever imagined that everyone on board a sinking ship would need to be in lifeboats at the same time. The lifeboat regulations were changed for the better in 1913.

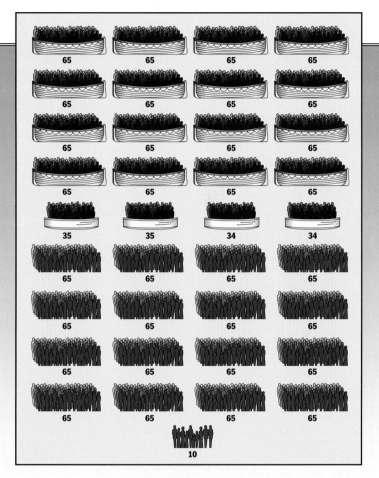

If the 16 lifeboats and 4 life rafts on the Titanic *had been filled to capacity (as seen at the top of this chart), 1,178 people could have been saved — but 1,050 people would have remained without hope of a seat.*

2:18 A.M.

Many of the *Titanic's* electrical systems as well as a few still-functioning boilers are now exposed to seawater. The ship's lights go out.

The *Titanic's* stern moves into an almost perpendicular position.

The great ship snaps into two pieces, breaking between the third and fourth funnels.

The bow plunges down at a sloping angle. There is a

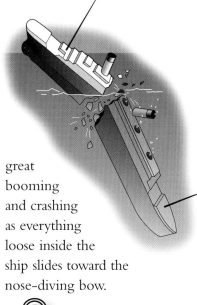

great booming and crashing as everything loose inside the ship slides toward the nose-diving bow.

2:19 A.M.

The bow has vanished.

For a moment, the stern settles back on the water, then tips forward, the propellers pointing at the sky.

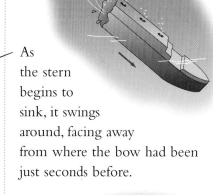

As the stern begins to sink, it swings around, facing away from where the bow had been just seconds before.

2:20 A.M.

In darkness, about 400 miles (645 km) southeast of Newfoundland, Canada, the *Titanic* sinks.

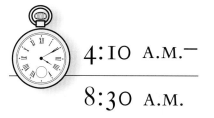

4:10 A.M.

8:30 A.M.

In the early hours of the morning on April 15, the *Carpathia* arrives.

Seven hundred and five survivors come aboard the ship from lifeboats. One thousand, five hundred and twenty-three lives have been lost.

37

THE TITANIC'S GIFTS

Word of the sea disaster spread quickly. The public was shocked to learn that the largest ship ever built was gone, and with it more than 1,500 lives.

Pride in the *Titanic's* size and majesty vanished and was replaced by sorrow. Confidence in technology and the amazing inventions it had helped to create was badly shaken. Only questions remained. How could the *Titanic* sink? Why did this tragedy happen?

Two inquiries, one American and one British, were set up to investigate. Dozens of

The Titanic disaster was front-page news in newspapers around the world.

people — from the White Star Line's chairman to wireless inventor Guglielmo Marconi, passengers, and crew — answered questions. The ship's construction, the use of the radio, the sinking of the ship, and the existing safety regulations were all explored. Investigators listened to the testimony for weeks, then thought about what they had heard. Finally, they presented their conclusions, including several recommendations designed to ensure that no similar tragedy ever occurred.

Here are some examples of how ocean travel was made safer as a result of their suggestions:

1 In 1913, an organization called the International Ice Patrol (IIP) was created. It is responsible for locating, tracking, and predicting the movements of icebergs in the North Atlantic. Traveling along the tracklines recommended by the IIP was made mandatory for all Atlantic steamships and enforced by governments.

In 1969, the IIP began to publish the "Limits of All Known Ice." If mariners stay outside this boundary drawn on the ocean, they should not encounter any ice.

To this day the Ice Patrol continues its successful efforts. Now Coast Guard aircraft use trained observers and radar to detect icebergs of any size, even in weather conditions in which the human eye can see

Collisions with icebergs are not a real danger for ships today. Coast Guard aircraft locate icebergs for the International Ice Patrol. Additional data on wind and weather are gathered, then the range and distribution of icebergs are plotted. Ships are then advised of safe areas in the Atlantic in which to travel.

almost nothing. This information is mapped on marine charts by a central IIP computer and passed on twice a day by radio broadcasts to ships in the Atlantic.

2 Shipbuilding specifications were changed to ensure that ships' keels would be stronger. Almost immediately after the *Titanic* sank, its sister ship *Olympic* was refitted. Its double hull was extended up the sides of the ship to 10 feet (3 m) above the waterline. As well, the *Olympic*'s watertight bulkheads were extended higher and sealed at the top. Today, the bulkheads on all ships are

required to be truly watertight. Instead of being open on the top like the *Titanic*'s "ice-cube tray" compartments, bulkheads must extend up to a higher deck that acts like a lid on the ship's compartments, ensuring that they are fully enclosed. Bulkheads must also be fireproof.

3 After the sinking of the *Titanic*, on-board safety regulations were rapidly improved, and they continue to be updated on a regular basis. Today, regulations ensure that there are enough

lifeboats and rafts for everyone on a ship and 25 percent more. Inflatable life rafts are stored on deck in containers no bigger than a lawn tractor. These rafts can each carry 40 to 60 people. If the ship sinks before the life rafts are launched, they automatically inflate and float to the surface.

Ships must have fire exit signs, public-address systems, and hallway alarms. Safety drills must be conducted within 24 hours of leaving port. Recently added safety features include low-level emergency lighting in the hallways (to help people if they must crawl through smoke-filled passages) and electronic heat and smoke detectors hooked up to a central computer system. When an alarm is triggered, the problem area can be quickly pinpointed on the central computer screen. Emergency help can be sent immediately and the area can be shut off from the rest of the ship until the problem is solved or help arrives.

Fireproof bulkheads that are truly watertight are now mandatory on ships.

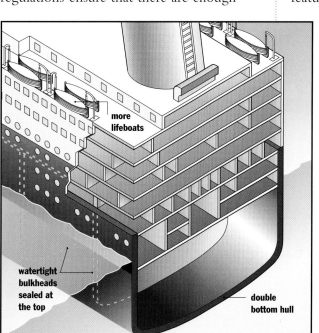

more lifeboats

watertight bulkheads sealed at the top

double bottom hull

From St. Pierre, a French island in the North Atlantic off the south coast of Newfoundland, Le Suroit *heads out toward the site of the* Titanic *disaster.*

THE SEARCH FOR THE TITANIC

Big isn't always better. Never underestimate the forces of nature. These are lessons that many people learned from the *Titanic* tragedy. Before the great ship sailed, there was a growing belief that science and technology could solve every problem.

The *Titanic*'s sinking reminded people that nature cannot be controlled by human beings and that, when people climb aboard vessels or vehicles to venture across water, across land, or into the air, there is always some element of risk. Nevertheless, science and technology continued to develop — and it is thanks to modern-day technology that scientists have been able to locate and learn more about the *Titanic*.

Many of the unanswered questions about the disaster could only be resolved by getting a good look at the ship. But finding the *Titanic* was not easy. Several expeditions were unsuccessful.

Then, in 1985, Robert Ballard and his team from the Woods Hole Oceanographic Institution in Massachusetts teamed up with a group of French scientists who had developed a revolutionary new side-scanning sonar, *sonar acoustique remorqué* (SAR).

The sonar equipment, towed behind the French ship *Le Suroit,* aimed sound signals at the ocean floor. When the sound waves hit something — whether the ocean floor or a shipwreck — they bounced back.

The sonar scanned in very wide sweeps — three-fifths of a mile (almost 1 km) wide — and its reflected echoes provided the scientists with a very detailed picture of

The Knorr lowers Argo, a submersible robot carrying video cameras, over the side and down to the ocean floor to search for the wreck of the Titanic.

the ocean floor. The scientists worked aboard *Le Suroit* for six weeks, from the beginning of July until mid-August 1985, covering almost three-quarters of their 150-square-mile (400 km²) search area, but they failed to find the *Titanic*. (They would later realize that they had passed within 100 yards [90 m] of it.) Their time was up. *Le Suroit* was needed elsewhere and had to leave the hunt.

On August 22, Ballard's team sailed out on the research vessel *Knorr* to explore the remainder of the *Le Suroit* search area and expand the search further. The *Knorr* towed an underwater unmanned robot, called *Argo*, that traveled just above the ocean floor. *Argo* was controlled by the research scientists aboard the *Knorr,* and its floodlights, video cameras, and forward-looking sonar acted as their eyes and ears.

The team searched for the *Titanic* for several days, with no luck. Suddenly, just after midnight on September 1, at a depth of 12,460 feet (3798 m), *Argo* detected small chunks of metal. Back on the surface, excitement began to build. These objects were definitely made by humans. Then — could it be? *Argo's* cameras relayed pictures of what the sonar had picked up, showing the crew something that appeared to be a boiler. It was circular, and it was massive — obviously made for a giant ship.

Just to be sure, one of the team members studied a 1911 photograph of one of the *Titanic's* boilers. The boiler in the photo matched the image appearing on the *Knorr's* computer screen. This was the *Titanic!*

Eagerly, the scientists watched the screen as *Argo* traveled on. Six hundred feet (200 m) later, more boilers and great pieces of the liner itself were seen — for the first time in more than 73 years.

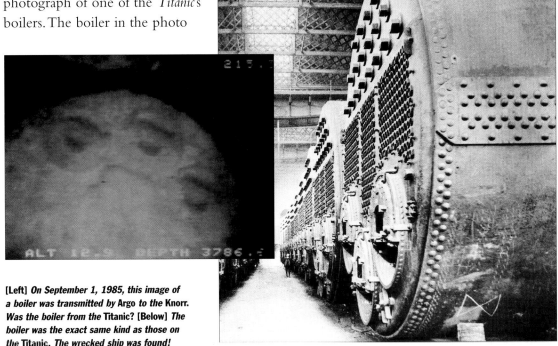

[Left] *On September 1, 1985, this image of a boiler was transmitted by* Argo *to the Knorr. Was the boiler from the* Titanic? [Below] *The boiler was the exact same kind as those on the* Titanic. *The wrecked ship was found!*

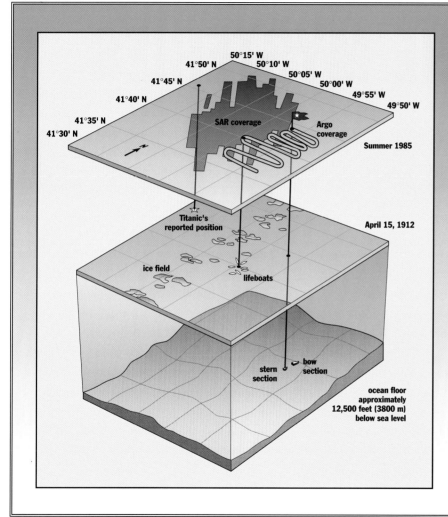

50°15' W
50°10' W
50°05' W
41°50' N
50°00' W
41°45' N
49°55' W
41°40' N
49°50' W
41°35' N
41°30' N

SAR coverage

Argo coverage

Summer 1985

Titanic's reported position

April 15, 1912

ice field

lifeboats

stern section

bow section

ocean floor approximately 12,500 feet (3800 m) below sea level

THE SEARCH AREA

Robert Ballard reckoned that the same currents that had carried the *Titanic*'s lifeboats south and southeast would also have acted on the ship itself — and on any objects falling out of it — as it plunged more than 2 miles (3.2 km) to the bottom of the ocean. Instead of searching for the *Titanic*'s hull, Ballard decided to hunt for its trail of debris. He calculated that the trail of debris would be located north of where the ship's lifeboats were found and east of the last recorded sighting of the row of icebergs, and that it would be about 1 mile (1.6 km) long. He then concentrated his team's search efforts on a 100-mile (160 km) area indicated by these calculations.

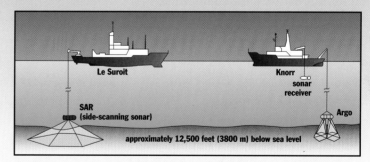

Le Suroit

Knorr

sonar receiver

SAR (side-scanning sonar)

Argo

approximately 12,500 feet (3800 m) below sea level

Le Suroit *searched unsuccessfully for the wreck using side-scanning sonar (SAR). The* Knorr, *searching farther east with the unmanned robot* Argo, *was successful.*

EXPLORING THE MYSTERIES

Now that the *Titanic* had been found, perhaps some of the mysteries surrounding it could be solved. First, the ship had to be examined in detail. For several more days in 1985, the submersible robot *Argo* explored the wreck. Robert Ballard directed the survey from above on the *Knorr*. The following summer, Ballard and his team returned to the *Titanic* with even more advanced equipment.

So far, the ship had been seen only in images taken by sonar and cameras. Now *Alvin,* a mini-submarine able to stay underwater for 12 hours at a time, took Ballard and two crew members down the 13,000 feet (4000 m) to the ocean floor. As *Alvin's* powerful electric lights sliced through the darkness of the ocean's depths, the team suddenly saw a huge wall of steel. It was the hull of the *Titanic.* They were looking at the great ship with their own eyes!

On later dives, *Alvin* was accompanied by *Jason Junior,* a small underwater robot that contained powerful lights, a color video camera, and a still camera. Known as the "swimming eyeball," *Jason Junior* was parked in front of *Alvin* in a basket-like garage and controlled remotely by the team inside *Alvin.* Attached to *Alvin* by a 250-foot (76 m) tether, *Jason Junior* could leave its garage to travel and maneuver right inside the wrecked ship. During the course of several dives, the robot took photographs outside and inside the ship. Photos were also taken by cameras aboard a submersible sled that was pulled back and forth 25 feet (8 m) above the *Titanic* by the *Knorr* and another research ship, the *Atlantis II.* These thousands of photos would prove very useful in learning more about the sinking of the *Titanic.*

Over the last few years, many scientific tests have been done on small pieces of the ship recovered from the wreck site. The results have been combined with other technical data on the ship and the visual information gathered by Ballard's explorations to answer some of the many questions still surrounding the great vessel.

Alvin's lights — here seen above the **Titanic's** *bow — penetrated the ocean depths to reveal ghostly relics such as a bench from the deck* [left] *and a statue of a Greek goddess from the first-class lounge* [right].

Mytery

Why was an iceberg able to sink the "unsinkable" Titanic?

No one aboard the *Titanic* got a good look at the damage done to the ship by the iceberg. Because of the speed at which the seawater poured in and the ship sank, it was commonly believed that the ship had received a huge, 300-foot (90 m) gash in its hull. When the wreck of the *Titanic* was finally discovered, everyone hoped that it would be possible to take photographs of the damage to the hull. But this proved to be impossible. The bow of the ship had driven deep into the ocean floor, hiding the iceberg damage beneath 50 feet (15 m) of mud.

Many people couldn't accept that an iceberg could slice through a hull that was made of 1-inch- (2.5 cm) thick steel. Could there have been a flaw in the steel used to make the *Titanic*'s hull?

Tests were done in the late 1980s and early 1990s on samples of hull plate retrieved from the wreck. Analysts concluded that, compared to today's steel, the steel used to make the *Titanic*'s hull was very brittle. The best steel is strong, yet flexible. Brittle steel, on the other hand, could crack or shatter in cold water, especially if anything struck it. Some scientists think that if the steel used in the *Titanic* had been of better quality and more flexible, the hull would not have broken as it scraped the iceberg. Instead, the ship would simply have bounced off.

However, there is no reason to think that the *Titanic*'s steel was of lesser quality than the steel used to make any other liner at that time. The steelmakers of 1912 made steel with the most up-to-date technology they had. If the theory that the hull steel was too brittle is correct, this means simply that the metallurgical science of the day could not keep up with engineering science. Engineers could build a huge vessel, but steelmakers could not yet make steel strong or flexible enough to keep such a titan in one piece after a brush with an iceberg.

There is another argument against the theory that the quality of the steel could be responsible for the sinking of the ship. If the steel was weak, the *Titanic*'s hull

The Titanic's hull plates were 6 feet (1.8 m) wide and almost 30 feet (9 m) long, with a weight of about 3 tons (2.7 t) each. The largest weighed 4 1/4 tons (3.9 t). But was the hull steel strong enough?

would surely have shattered when it struck the ocean floor. Yet in 1996, a French expedition found that the port (left) side of the ship — the side that didn't strike the iceberg — had crumpled, not shattered, when the ship hit bottom.

Mystery

Did the Titanic's seams pop?

In 1996, *Titanic* investigators used sound waves to penetrate the thick mud surrounding the hull and create an ultrasound image of the *Titanic's* side. Instead of the huge gash that many expected to find, the ultrasound revealed six separate, thin tears in the side of the ship. This discovery led to new theories that the wrought-iron rivets used

to hold the steel plates together had been the weak link that caused the ship to sink.

When the *Titanic's* hull scraped along the iceberg, the pressure on the outside of the hull plates would have caused them to bend inward. This, in turn, would have put pressure on the rivets holding together the hull plates. If the rivet heads were weak, they would have simply popped off. The pressure of the iceberg, and then of the seawater, would have forced the plates to separate, making openings through which the water could pour.

Marine analysts have examined two rivets taken from the *Titanic's* hull. These two rivets contain unusually high amounts of slag — a glassy material left behind in iron during the process used to separate it from ore. Some slag in iron is useful,

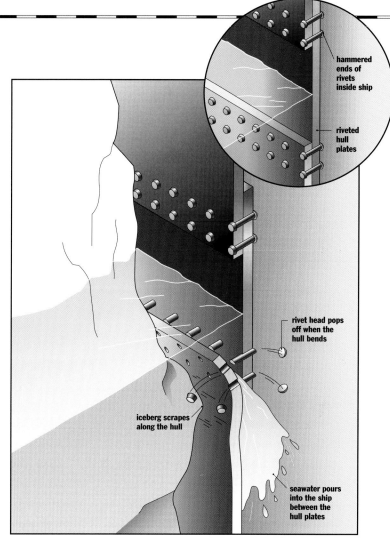

hammered ends of rivets inside ship

riveted hull plates

rivet head pops off when the hull bends

iceberg scrapes along the hull

seawater pours into the ship between the hull plates

[Above] *The* Titanic's *hull, intact.* [Below] *Is this what happened when the* Titanic's *hull plates met the iceberg? Were the rivet heads the weakest link in the hull's strength? Perhaps they could not hold together the bending steel.*

because it makes the iron stronger. Too much slag can make iron brittle. Were the two rivets tested similar to the millions of other rivets used to build the ship, or is it possible that they belonged to only a handful of flawed ones? *Titanic* investigators hope to obtain more rivets from the wreck and do further testing to help answer these questions.

High slag content is not the only way the rivets might have been weakened. The rivets may well have been of top quality when they were manufactured, but perhaps the riveters working on the *Titanic* occasionally left the rivets in the furnace too long. Instead of removing the rivets when they were red hot, they may have allowed them to overheat and become white hot. The overheated metal would have become much more brittle — too brittle to hold together hull plates under pressure from an iceberg and seawater.

Or, perhaps the rivets were of top quality but simply unable to hold the *Titanic* together against the iceberg. There are still many unanswered questions about the rivets.

Mystery

Did the Titanic go down unbroken?

Eyewitnesses gave differing accounts of the ship's sinking. Some said the ship split into two pieces before sinking. Others claimed it went down in one nose-diving piece. With the help of modern technology, the truth is gradually being discovered.

Scientists now know that the *Titanic* broke apart before sinking. *Argo's* cameras revealed that the *Titanic* is in two pieces on the ocean floor, with a central piece missing altogether. Many surviving passengers had reported that, before the ship sank, the stern lifted up and pointed directly into the sky. Computer reconstructions now confirm that the *Titanic* was almost vertical before it sank.

This incredible position — with the heavy stern forced into the air — put tremendous stress on the ship's hull. The reconstructions of the sinking have demonstrated that the weight of the almost-upright stern would have caused the ship to begin breaking apart at the water's surface, finally snapping in two between the third and fourth funnels, three-fifths of the way from the front of the ship. Photographs from *Argo* show that the bow did break from the stern about three-fifths of the way along the ship.

The stress on the ship would also have caused severe bending at the ship's two expansion joints (hinges in the topmost decks made to bend and flex in rough seas). One of these joints was positioned right between the third and fourth funnels.

As the ship split, shreds of hull plate from both sides of the rupture detached and sank, landing apart from the bow and stern. Some of these large sections of plate have been seen on the ocean floor at the wreck site.

Could something other than the stress of its vertical position have caused the ship to break into pieces? Passengers claim to have heard rumblings and explosions before the ship sank. It may be that one or more of the red-hot boilers that had remained working exploded like a bomb when touched by the cold seawater entering the sinking ship and ripped the hull apart.

The bow sank before the stern did. It didn't plunge straight to the bottom of the ocean and hit head-on. Instead, it traveled downward at a sloping angle, and when it reached the sea bottom, it dug into it on a similar gentle angle, plowing about 100 feet (30 m) before stopping.

After the bow and sections of hull plate had vanished, the *Titanic*'s stern settled back to a horizontal position. It remained afloat only a few seconds longer. The ship's massive engines, bolted firmly into the ship's floor, were near the broken section of the ship. The weight of the engines and the water pouring in tipped the stern section forward. The propellers at the end of the ship were now pointing to the sky. As the stern began to sink, it swung around, facing away from the bow. Still loaded down with the three huge engines, the stern plummeted straight down, ending up 1,970 feet (600 m) away from the bow. Objects spilled out of the ship during its descent, covering the ocean floor between the bow and the stern. The *Titanic* was gone.

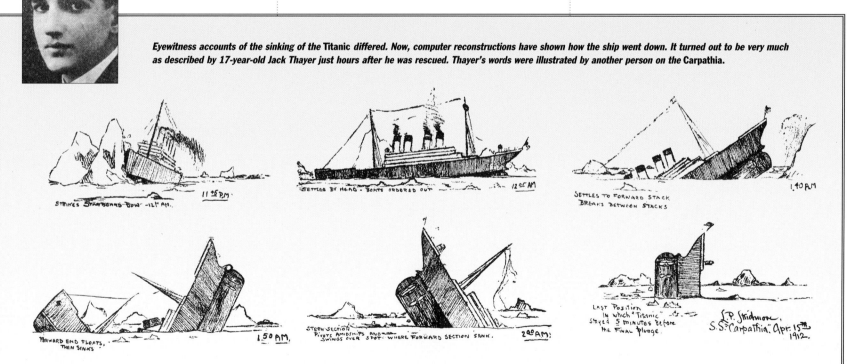

Eyewitness accounts of the sinking of the Titanic *differed. Now, computer reconstructions have shown how the ship went down. It turned out to be very much as described by 17-year-old Jack Thayer just hours after he was rescued. Thayer's words were illustrated by another person on the* Carpathia.

A LIVING SHIP

Interest in the *Titanic* continues today, almost nine decades after the sinking of the ship. Many hundreds of artifacts have been plundered from the site of the wreck — cups plates, light fixtures, even a bathtub. Coal that spilled out onto the ocean floor during the *Titanic*'s plunge to the bottom is now being advertised for sale on the Internet. There has been a blockbuster movie based on the ship's dramatic story, and visitors still come to see the rows of graves of the drowned passengers at a cemetery in Halifax, Nova Scotia. Submarine trips to the shipwreck are now available for tourists, and replicas of the *Titanic* are being built, so that a new generation of passengers can complete the ship's never-finished maiden voyage.

This pocket watch, damaged by seawater, stopped just 15 minutes after the Titanic sank.

The pride of the White Star Line was indeed a titan, but its massive size could not save it from an iceberg. The most advanced technology was used to build the ship and protect it at sea — but it was built and navigated by human beings. Human beings operated the radio and failed to pass on important ice warnings to the officers. They decided how to steer the ship after the iceberg was sighted. They made the rivets that were to hold the ship's plates together. They decided that the *Titanic*'s double bottom hull need not extend up its sides above the waterline. And they did not make the ship's compartments truly watertight.

To relive the night of the *Titanic*'s sinking in 1912 is to relive a night of sorrow. But the story does not end there. The doomed ship left behind valuable lessons. One was a reminder that, although humans can create marvelous technological masterpieces, technology is a tool that must be used wisely. Another was to respect the unpredictable power of nature. The tragedy also resulted in safer regulations and practices for ships that sail the seas today.

The *Titanic* is gone, but it is not forgotten. There is no doubt that the beautiful ocean liner lives on in our imaginations.

GLOSSARY

Bow. The front of a ship.

Bridge. The structure on a ship from which the captain and officers direct operations.

Bulkhead. An upright partition or wall separating the compartments on a ship

Crow's-nest. A platform or enclosure for a lookout, located on the mast of a ship.

Dry dock. An enclosed dock that can be emptied of water and in which ships are built or repaired.

Fitting-out dock. A dock, usually at a shipyard, for "fitting out" or adding parts and equipment to complete a new ship.

Foremast. The mast at the front of a ship.

Framing. The process of constructing the rigid supporting structures, or ribs, of a ship.

Gantry. A towerlike metal framework that supports a moving crane.

Generating engine. An engine used to produce electricity.

Hull. The outer shell of a ship.

Inquiry. A formal investigation into a matter of public concern.

Keel. The main lengthwise steel structure, or backbone, of a ship, which supports the framework of the ship's hull.

Knot. One knot is equal to a speed of one nautical mile (which is about 2,025 yards [1852 m] per hour).

Morse code. A system of dashes and dots that represent letters in the alphabet. Created in 1901 and named after its inventor, Samuel Morse.

Paddle wheel. A wheel with blades fitted around its circumference. When revolved, the blades push against the water and move the boat forward.

Piston. The driving mechanism(s) within the cylinder(s) of an engine, put in motion by the addition of steam or other gas under pressure.

Port. The left-hand side (looking forward) of a ship.

Quartermaster. The officer in charge of steering the ship and signaling.

Quarters. The crew accommodation or any assigned location or station aboard ship.

Reciprocating engine. An engine using pistons moving up and down in cylinders. ("Reciprocate" means to go with an alternating backward and forward motion. The motion of the pistons gave this type of engine its name.)

Rivet. A bolt-like fastener inserted through a drilled hole and hammered or pressed flat to hold steel plates together.

Rudder. A flat piece hinged vertically to the stern of a ship for use in steering.

Slipway. An inclined slope upon which ships are built.

Starboard. The right-hand side (looking forward) of a ship.

Submersible. A submarine operating under the water, usually for short time periods and for purposes of exploration.

Turbine engine. A rotary engine driven by a flow of water, gas, wind, or steam over blades.

Waterline. The line along which the surface of the water touches the side of a ship.

Wheelhouse. The structure on a ship that contains the steering wheel.

Wireless. A radio system that does not require wires to transmit signals.